S0-BUB-633

This book belongs to

ELIANA

DSI MADERA

SAN CARLOS

REED

Reed Publishing (NZ) Ltd
Te Karuhi tā tāpui o Reed (Aotearoa)

Established in 1907, Reed is New Zealand's largest
book publisher, with over 300 titles in print.

For details on all these books visit our website:
www.reed.co.nz

Published by Reed Children's Books, a division of Reed Publishing (NZ) Ltd,
39 Rawene Rd, Birkenhead, Auckland 10. Associated companies, branches
and representatives throughout the world.

This book is copyright. Except for the purpose of fair reviewing, no part of
this publication may be reproduced or transmitted in any form or by any
means, electronic or mechanical, including photocopying, recording, or any
information storage and retrieval system, without permission in writing from
the publisher. Infringers of copyright render themselves liable to prosecution.

© 2004 Bob Darroch
The author asserts his moral rights in the work.

National Library of New Zealand Cataloguing-in-Publication Data
Darroch, Bob, 1940-
Little Kiwi looks after the egg / written and illustrated by Bob
Darroch.
ISBN 1-8694-8664-1
[1. Kiwis—Fiction. 2. Eggs—Fiction. 3. Animals—Infancy—
Fiction. 4. Birds—New Zealand—Fiction.] I. Title.
NZ823.2—dc 21

ISBN 1 86948 664 1
First published 2004

Printed in China

LITTLE KIWI
LOOKS AFTER
THE EGG

written and illustrated by
BOB DARROCH

'Little Kiwi!' called Mum. 'Your dad needs my help for a minute. Can you come and look after the egg, please?'
'Sure,' Little Kiwi replied, 'but why does it need looking after? It's just an egg, isn't it?'
Mum smiled. 'It's much more than just an egg,' she said. 'Very soon a little brother or sister will hatch out, just the way you did. It's very important that we keep this egg nice and safe. We can't let anything happen to it.'

Little Kiwi felt very important. He would make sure that the egg stayed safe until Mum got back.

'I wonder what it will be like having a brother or a sister,' he thought. 'That could be fun!'

Then, as he dreamed, the egg started to wobble and a sharp little

knock,
    knock,
        knock

came from inside.

A tiny little hole had appeared in the side of the egg.

'Er … hello,' Little Kiwi called shyly.

'Hello,' a voice answered. 'Who are you?'

'I'm your big brother,' Little Kiwi answered.

'Hello, big brother!' said the voice. 'I'd invite you in but I can't seem to find the door.'

'There's no door,' laughed Little Kiwi. 'You have to push until the shell breaks.'

The egg started bouncing around until — **kachonk!** — out popped two feet. 'What are those things?' asked the egg. 'Oh, those are feet,' Little Kiwi replied. 'They're great things to have,' he told the egg. 'With them you can jump and dance …'

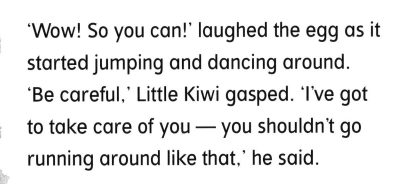

'Wow! So you can!' laughed the egg as it started jumping and dancing around. 'Be careful,' Little Kiwi gasped. 'I've got to take care of you — you shouldn't go running around like that,' he said.

Straight away, Little Kiwi realised he shouldn't have mentioned running.
'You mean you can run with these feet things?' said the egg.
'Hey, running sounds like fun,' and with that the egg took off.
'Wait! Stop!' Little Kiwi wailed. 'I'm meant to be taking care of you!
Oh no,' he moaned, 'now we're in trouble,' and he took off after
the egg.

Leaves and sticks flew everywhere as the egg
zoomed through the forest.
'What was that?' squawked a startled weka as the
sprinting egg shot through her nest.

'Sorry,' Little Kiwi panted as he followed. 'That's my egg — I'm meant to be looking after it.'
'Looks more like you're *running* after it,' she huffed. 'What a hoon!'

The egg came to — and through — a stream.
'Oh man,' muttered Little Kiwi. He didn't really like water but he had to keep the egg safe, so through he went.
'Crazy hoons!' spluttered a kingfisher on a tree branch as the water showered down on top on him.

'Oh no!' moaned Little Kiwi as the egg belted along a log bridge over a waterfall.

He'd never been brave enough to cross here before but he had to keep that crazy egg safe. So with his eyes tightly closed he wobbled across the log.

He opened his eyes just in time to see the egg heading for another log bridge — this one ending in mid-air, halfway across the stream. **'Stop!'** he yelled.

Too late!

The egg sprinted off the end of the log and bounced off the back of a heron that was flying past.
The heron crashed into the water while the egg landed safely, still running, on the riverbank.
'Oh man! Oh man!' Little Kiwi groaned. 'How am I ever going to keep this egg safe?'

He bounded along the log and tried to jump to the other
side, but couldn't quite jump that far.

As the soggy heron was taking off again — **kaboing**!
— Little Kiwi bounced to the riverbank and the heron hit
the water again.

The heron muttered something about hoons and decided
to walk home.

Now where was the egg?
From a clump of bushes came a loud startled squawk.
Little Kiwi didn't really like rushing into strange dark places, but he had to catch up with the egg.
He rushed in and found a very ruffled, very surprised pukeko flat on her back.
'What was that?' she stammered.
'My egg,' spluttered Little Kiwi. 'I'm meant to be looking after it.'
'Well, it's a hoon!' Pukeko told him as she scrambled back out of the bushes.

Tired out, Little Kiwi staggered on, following a trail of scattered, fluttering leaves — and scattered, fluttering birds.

'What on earth am I going to tell Mum?'
he panted. 'I told her I'd look after this egg.'

At last the trail led back to the burrow. There was the egg,
lying quietly at the back of the nest.
Little Kiwi gently lifted the shell off and gazed down at
the tiny kiwi lying there.
A sister!
Totally exhausted he flopped down beside her and
promptly fell asleep.

'Ah, isn't that lovely!' beamed Mum when she came home.
'What a good big brother you are, taking such good care of your little sister.'

'**W**on't it be fun to have a little sister to play with?' Mum said.

'You'll be able to look after her and take her for nice quiet
walks in the bush!'

Little Kiwi was too tired to answer.

All he could do was mutter, 'Oh man!'

About the author

Bob Darroch has been a freelance cartoonist and illustrator for a number of years. He started writing and illustrating his own books for children in 1999 with the release of *The Kiwi That Was Scared of the Dark* and followed this up in 2002 with *The Kiwi That Lost His Mum*.

Bob lives in Temuka and is married with two children and two grandsons.

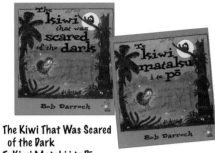

The Kiwi That Was Scared of the Dark
Te Kiwi Mataki i te Pō
Bob Darroch

It's night and Little Kiwi is out for his first walk with his mum. The only problem is that the night is full of scary noises and he's terrified of the dark! He meets other night creatures but that doesn't help. What happens when he decides to venture out during the day? Also available in Maori.

The Kiwi That Lost His Mum
Bob Darroch

When little Kiwi hatches from his egg, an accident launches him out into the world on an unexpected adventure. He's got to get back home to Mum but can't really remember what she looks like!

Little Kiwi Meets a Monster
Bob Darroch

Little Kiwi is going foraging at night with his dad — into a part of the bush he has never been to before. While Dad is busy collecting worms and grubs, Little Kiwi meets a terrifying monster — or does he?! Soon the bush is in an uproar and Little Kiwi must face up to his fears.

Is It Time to Get Up Yet?
Bob Darroch

All parents are familiar with the cry 'Is it time to get up yet?' In this fun, lively book, this familiar refrain becomes a hilarious view of having to stay in bed. Imagination runs riot and in the end the young hero of the story is just plain worn out!

REED